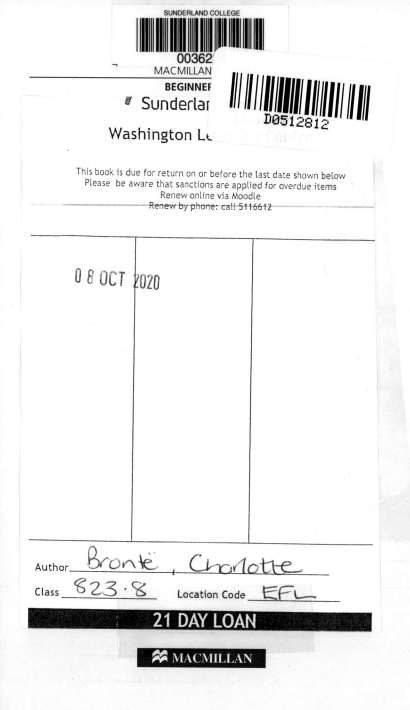

BEGINNER LEVEL

Founding Editor: John Milne

The Macmillan Readers provide a choice of enjoyable reading materials for learners of English. The series is published at six levels – Starter, Beginner, Elementary, Pre-intermediate, Intermediate and Upper.

Level control
Information, structure and vocabulary are controlled to suit the students' ability at each level.

The number of words at each level:

Starter	about 300 basic words
Beginner	about 600 basic words
Elementary	about 1100 basic words
Pre-intermediate	about 1400 basic words
Intermediate	about 1600 basic words
Upper	about 2200 basic words

Vocabulary
Some difficult words and phrases in this book are important for understanding the story. Some of these words are explained in the story and some are shown in the pictures. From Pre-intermediate level upwards, words are marked with a number like this: ...^{3}. These words are explained in the Glossary at the end of the book.

Contents

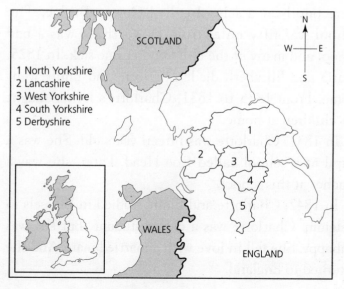

1 North Yorkshire
2 Lancashire
3 West Yorkshire
4 South Yorkshire
5 Derbyshire

SCOTLAND

WALES

ENGLAND

A Note About the Author

Charlotte Brontë was born on 21st April 1816. She lived in the village of Haworth, in West Yorkshire, in the north of England. Her father was a clergyman. He worked in the church at Haworth.

Charlotte had four sisters. They were Maria, Elizabeth, Emily and Anne. Charlotte had one brother – Branwell. Charlotte was not pretty and her eyes were weak. But Charlotte was clever and she had a strong character.

In 1824, Maria, Elizabeth, Charlotte and Emily were pupils at a school called Cowan Bridge. The school was fifty miles from Haworth. It was a bad school and many of the children became sick. In 1825, Maria and Elizabeth died. Charlotte and Emily went home. From 1825 to 1831, Charlotte's father taught his children at home.

In 1831, Charlotte was fifteen years old. She was a pupil at a school called Roe Head. Later, she was a teacher at this school.

In 1842, Charlotte and Emily studied in Brussels in Belgium. Charlotte was a clever student. But she was unhappy. She fell in love with a married man. And she returned to England.

Charlotte, Emily, Anne and Branwell wrote stories and they drew pictures. They also wrote poetry. Branwell was going to be an artist. But he became ill. He drank alcohol and he took drugs.

The Brontë sisters sent their stories to a publisher. In the 1850s, women's stories were not often published. So Charlotte wrote her books with the name, Currer Bell. Emily wrote *Wuthering Heights* with the name, Ellis Bell. And Anne wrote *Agnes Grey* with the name, Acton Bell. Their books were very popular. Soon people wanted to meet these authors. Then they were surprised. These good writers were women!

Charlotte Brontë's novels are: *The Professor, Jane Eyre* (1847), *Shirley* (1849) and *Villette* (1853). *Jane Eyre* is one of the most popular stories in English. In 1847, people read *Jane Eyre* and they were surprised. Women did not often speak about their hopes and their thoughts. Women did not talk to men in this way!

In 1848, Emily and Branwell died. Anne died the next year. Charlotte lived with her old father. She was now a famous author. People wanted to meet her. Charlotte travelled to London and she met poets, artists and writers. She visited theatres, museums and art galleries. In 1854, Charlotte married a clergyman, Arthur Nicholls. On 31st March 1855, Charlotte Brontë died. She was 38 years old.

A Note About This Story

Time: The 1830s. **Place:** The north of England.

Early in the nineteenth century, there were no cars or trains. People rode horses. People travelled in coaches or in carriages pulled by horses. Journeys were long and difficult. Most people lived in the countryside. Rich people had large houses and many servants.

Rich children learnt their lessons in their homes. A teacher lived in their house. Some poor children lived at their schools. Some of these schools were very bad. The buildings were cold and uncomfortable. These children did not have enough food. Their teachers often beat them.

The Brontës were poor. The three sisters worked as governesses. Governesses lived in the homes of rich families. They taught the children of these families.

In the story, *Jane Eyre*, Charlotte Brontë wrote about her own life. Jane was unhappy in a bad school. Charlotte was unhappy too. Jane Eyre was not pretty. But she was clever and she was good. Charlotte was not pretty. But she was intelligent and she worked hard. In the story, Jane Eyre becomes a governess. Charlotte was a governess in the homes of two rich families. She hated the work.

In 1851, there were about 25000 governesses in England. Many poor women from good families worked as governesses. They were not married. Governesses were not paid well.

The People in This Story

Jane Eyre
dʒeɪn ˈeə

Aunt Reed
ɑːnt ˈriːd

Mr Brocklehurst
mɪstə ˈbrɒklhɜːst

Mrs Fairfax
mɪsɪz ˈfeəfæks

Adèle Varens
ˈædel ˈværæns

Grace Poole
greɪs ˈpuːl

Edward Rochester
ˈedwəd ˈrɒtʃɪstə

Richard Mason
ˈrɪtʃəd ˈmeɪsən

Bertha Mason
ˈbɜːθə ˈmeɪsən

Diana Rivers
daɪˈjænə ˈrɪvəz

Mary Rivers
ˈmeərɪ ˈrɪvəz

St John Rivers
ˈsɪndʒən ˈrɪvəz

1

My Story Begins

In 1825, I was ten years old. My father and mother were dead. I lived with my aunt and uncle, Mr and Mrs Reed. Their house was called Gateshead Hall. The house was in Yorkshire, in the north of England. My Aunt and Uncle Reed had two children – a boy, John, and a girl, Eliza.

I liked my Uncle Reed and he liked me. But in 1825, my uncle died. After that, I was very unhappy. My Aunt Reed did not like me. And John and Eliza were unkind to me.

It was a cold, rainy day in December. All of us were in the house. I wanted to be alone. I wanted to read. I opened a book. Then I heard my Cousin John's voice.

'Jane! Jane Eyre! Where are you?' John shouted. He came into the room and he saw me.

'Why are you reading my book?' he asked. 'Give it to me!'

John took the book. He hit my head with it. I screamed. John hit me again. I pulled his hair and I kicked him.

'Help! Help, Mamma!' John shouted. 'Jane Eyre is hurting me!'

Aunt Reed ran into the room. She pulled me away from John.

'John hit me with a book,' I said. 'I hate him. And I hate you too!'

'You are a bad girl, Jane,' my aunt said. 'Why do you hate me?'

'You don't like me,' I replied. 'John and Eliza are unkind to me. I want to leave Gateshead Hall.'

'You want to leave!' Aunt Reed said. 'Where will you go? Your parents are dead. You cannot live alone.'

Aunt Reed thought for a moment.

'My friend, Mr Brocklehurst, is the owner of a school,' she said. 'I will send you to Mr Brocklehurst's school.'

———

A few days later, Mr Brocklehurst came to Gateshead Hall. He was a very tall man. His eyes were dark and his face was cruel.

'Jane Eyre,' he said to me. 'God does not like bad children. God punishes bad children, Jane Eyre.'

'God will punish John Reed,' I replied. 'John Reed hits me and he shouts at me.'

'That is not true. You are a liar, Jane Eyre,' Mr Brocklehurst said. 'You must not tell lies. And you must not live here with your cousins. You will come to Lowood School. You will become a good girl.'

'I want to come to your school, sir,' I said. 'I want to leave this house.'

'Bad girls are punished at my school, Jane Eyre,' Mr Brocklehurst said. 'The girls work very hard at Lowood.'

'I will work hard. I will be a good pupil, Mr Brocklehurst,' I said.

Two weeks later, I left Gateshead Hall. I went to Lowood School.

2

Lowood School

It was the month of January. I arrived at Lowood School at night. A servant took me up some stairs and into a big bedroom. There were many beds in the room. The girls in the beds were asleep. The servant took me to an empty bed. I put on my nightclothes and I got into bed. Soon, I was asleep too.

I woke up very early. A loud bell was ringing. The bedroom was dark and cold. I watched the other girls. They washed in cold water and they dressed quickly.

There was a plain brown dress next to my bed. And there was a pair of ugly, heavy shoes. I washed quickly. Then I put on my new clothes.

I was very hungry. I followed the other girls down the stairs. We sat down at long tables in a large dining-room. Our food was terrible.

'The food is bad again,' one of the girls said.

'Stand up!' a teacher shouted. 'Don't talk!'

We stood up. We did not speak. We walked into a big schoolroom and we sat down.

There were about eighty girls in the schoolroom. And there were four classes. The oldest girls were in the fourth class. I was in the first class.

Four teachers came into the room and we began our lessons. The lessons were not interesting. First, we read some pages in a book. Then our teacher asked us questions about those pages.

After four hours, we went outside. It was very cold. Very soon, a bell rang. Lessons started again.

———

Three weeks passed. One afternoon, the head teacher came into the schoolroom. The head teacher's name was Miss Temple. Mr Brocklehurst was with her. We all stood up. I stood behind an older girl. I did not want Mr Brocklehurst to see me.

Mr Brocklehurst walked slowly round the room. Everybody was very quiet. And then I dropped my book!

Mr Brocklehurst stopped walking. He looked at me.

'Ah! The new girl,' he said. 'Come here, Jane Eyre!' Then he pointed at two of the older girls. 'You two girls – put Jane Eyre on that high chair!' he said.

'Look at Jane Eyre, everybody!' Mr Brocklehurst said. 'This child is bad. She is a liar. She will be punished! Miss Temple! Teachers! Girls! Do not talk to this child.'

Then he spoke to me again.

'Jane Eyre, you must stand on that chair for two hours,' he said. 'You are a bad girl!'

That evening, I cried and cried. But Miss Temple was kind to me.

'You are a good pupil, Jane,' she said. 'And you are not a bad girl. I am your friend, Jane.'

'Thank you, Miss Temple,' I said.

———

Lowood School was in an unhealthy place. The buildings were wet and cold. Mr Brocklehurst owned the school. He was a rich man. But he did not buy warm clothes for us. And he did not buy good food for us. Everybody hated him.

In the spring, many of the girls became sick. Some of them left the school. They never came back. Many of the girls died.

That spring was a terrible time. We had no lessons. Miss Temple and the other teachers took care of the sick pupils. Mr Brocklehurst had to buy better food for us. And he had to buy warm clothes for us. Mr Brocklehurst never came to the school.

––––––

The next year, Lowood School moved to a better place. It was a healthier place. There were new school-rooms, new bedrooms and a new dining-room. The new buildings were bright and clean. The teachers were happy. After that, I was happy at Lowood School too.

I was a pupil at Lowood School for six years. Then I became a teacher. I was a teacher at the school for two years. But I never returned to Gateshead Hall. And the Reeds never wrote to me.

3

Thornfield Hall

In 1833, I was eighteen years old. In the summer, Miss Temple left Lowood School. She got married. I wanted to leave Lowood too. I wanted a new life.

'I will be a governess,' I thought.

I put an advertisement in a newspaper.

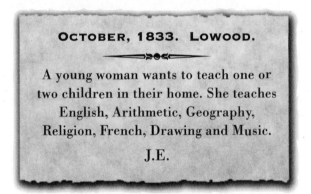

OCTOBER, 1833. LOWOOD.

A young woman wants to teach one or two children in their home. She teaches English, Arithmetic, Geography, Religion, French, Drawing and Music.

J.E.

I had a reply to my advertisement. The reply was from Mrs Fairfax of Thornfield Hall, near Millcote. Millcote was about seventy miles from Lowood School. Mrs Fairfax wanted a governess for a little girl.

I wrote to Mrs Fairfax immediately. I was going to be a governess at Thornfield Hall!

I travelled to Millcote in a coach. At Millcote, a servant met me. He took me to Thornfield Hall. At Thornfield Hall, another servant opened the door. She was smiling. She took me into a small, warm room. A lady was in the room. She was sitting by the fire.

'Are you Mrs Fairfax?' I asked her.

'Yes, my dear,' she said. 'And you are Miss Eyre. Are you cold? Sit by the fire, Miss Eyre. A servant will bring you some food.'

'Mrs Fairfax is very kind,' I said to myself. 'I will be happy here.'

'Will I see Miss Fairfax tonight?' I asked.

Mrs Fairfax looked at me. She smiled.

'Miss Fairfax? No, no,' she said. 'Your pupil's name is not Miss Fairfax. Your pupil is Adèle Varens. Adèle's mother was a Frenchwoman. Adèle is Mr Rochester's ward. He takes care of her.'

'Mr Rochester? Who is Mr Rochester?' I asked.

'Mr Edward Rochester is the owner of Thornfield Hall,' Mrs Fairfax said. 'I am his housekeeper. I take care of Thornfield Hall. Mr Rochester is not here now. He does not like this house. He is often away from home.'

I was very tired. Mrs Fairfax took me up the wide stairs. She took me to my room. I went to bed immediately. And I slept well.

———

The next morning, I woke early. The sun was shining. I put on a plain black dress. I opened my bedroom door. I walked along a corridor and down the wide stairs. I walked out into the sunny garden.

I turned and I looked up at my new home. Thornfield Hall was a beautiful house with many large windows. The garden was beautiful too.

After a few minutes, Mrs Fairfax came into the garden. She spoke to me.

'Good morning, Miss Eyre,' she said. 'You have woken early. Miss Adèle is here. After breakfast, you must take her to the schoolroom. She must begin her lessons.'

A pretty little girl walked towards me. She was about eight years old. She spoke to me in French and I replied in French.

After breakfast, I took Adèle to the schoolroom. We worked all morning. Adèle enjoyed her lessons and I was happy.

In the afternoon, Mrs Fairfax took me into all the rooms of Thornfield Hall. We looked at the paintings and at the beautiful furniture. We walked along the corridors.

'Come up onto the roof, Miss Eyre,' Mrs Fairfax said. 'You will see the beautiful countryside around Thornfield Hall.'

We walked up many stairs. At last, we were at the top of the house. We walked along the top corridor. Mrs Fairfax opened a small door and we walked onto the roof.

'Look, Miss Eyre,' Mrs Fairfax said. 'You can see for many miles.'

We stood on the roof for a few minutes. Then we went back into the house. We walked carefully towards the stairs. The top corridor was narrow and dark.

Suddenly, I heard a strange laugh.

'Who is that, Mrs Fairfax?' I asked.

Mrs Fairfax did not reply. She knocked on a door.

'Grace!' she said. The door opened. Behind the door was a small room. A servant was standing at the door.

'Be quiet, Grace, please,' Mrs Fairfax said.

The woman looked at Mrs Fairfax. Then she closed the door.

'That was Grace Poole,' Mrs Fairfax said. 'She works up here. Sometimes she laughs and talks with the other servants. Don't worry about Grace. Please come downstairs now, Miss Eyre.'

4

Mr Rochester

Three months passed. I had not met the owner of Thornfield Hall. Mr Rochester had not come home.

One January afternoon, I went out and I walked towards the road. I was going to the village of Hay. I was going to post a letter in the village. Hay was two miles from Thornfield Hall. The day was fine but it was very cold. I walked quickly and soon I was near the village.

Suddenly, a big black-and-white dog ran past me. A moment later, a man on a black horse followed the dog.

Then, I heard an angry shout. The dog ran past me again. It was barking loudly. I turned round. The horse had fallen on the icy ground and the man had fallen from the horse. I walked towards them.

'Can I help you, sir?' I asked.

'My horse fell. I've hurt my foot,' the man said.

The horse stood up. The man tried to stand up too. But he could not stand. He fell onto the ground again.

The man was about thirty-five years old. He was not handsome but he had a strong face. He had dark eyes and black hair. He was not very tall but his body was powerful.

'I'll bring somebody from Thornfield Hall,' I said.

'Do you live at Thornfield?' the man asked.

'I am the governess,' I replied.

'Ah, yes. The governess,' the man said. 'Help me, please.'

The man stood up very slowly, and he put his hand on my shoulder. He walked slowly towards his horse. I helped him. He pulled himself onto the horse.

'Thank you. Now go home quickly,' the man said. And he rode away.

I walked on to the village and I posted my letter. Then I returned to Thornfield Hall. Bright lights were shining in the big house. I went inside.

A big black-and-white dog walked towards me. It came from the dining-room. I had seen the dog before.

'Whose dog is that?' I asked a servant.

'It's Mr Rochester's dog,' the servant replied. 'Mr Rochester has come home. But he has hurt his foot. His horse fell on some ice.'

I smiled. The owner of Thornfield Hall had returned! But I did not see Mr Rochester again that day.

———

I saw Mr Rochester the next day. He sent for me in the evening. I put on a clean dress. I brushed my hair carefully.

Mr Rochester was in the large sitting-room. He was sitting in a big chair. His right foot was on a small chair. Mrs Fairfax and Adèle were sitting with him.

'This is Miss Eyre, sir,' Mrs Fairfax said.

Mr Rochester looked at me. He did not smile.

'Sit by the fire, Miss Eyre,' he said. 'Where have you come from?'

'From Lowood School,' I replied. 'I was there for eight years.'

'Eight years!' Mr Rochester said. 'That is a long time! Who are your parents?'

'I have no parents, sir,' I answered. 'They are dead.'

'But where is your home, Miss Eyre?' Mr Rochester asked.

'I have no home, sir. I have no family,' I said.

'Why did you come to Thornfield Hall?' Mr Rochester asked.

'I wanted to leave Lowood, sir,' I replied. 'I put an advertisement in a newspaper. Mrs Fairfax replied to my advertisement.'

'Yes, I did,' Mrs Fairfax said. 'Miss Eyre is a good teacher, Mr Rochester.'

Mr Rochester smiled for the first time.

'You are very young, Miss Eyre,' he said.

'I am eighteen, sir,' I replied.

Mr Rochester smiled again. He did not ask me more questions.

———

After that evening, I did not see Mr Rochester for a few days. Then, one night, he sent for me again.

'Sit near me, Miss Eyre,' he said. 'Mrs Fairfax will talk to Adèle.'

I sat down quietly, but I did not speak. The fire was very bright. I saw Mr Rochester's face clearly. I saw his large, dark eyes. He was smiling. He was happy.

After a minute, Mr Rochester spoke.

'Miss Eyre,' he said. 'You are looking at me very carefully. Am I a handsome man?'

'No, sir,' I said.

'You speak the truth, Miss Eyre!' Mr Rochester said. 'Look at me again. Am I a kind man?'

'No, sir,' I said again. 'You are smiling now. But you are not always kind.'

'That is true,' Mr Rochester replied. 'I have had a difficult life. I have met bad people. I have been a bad person myself. Now Thornfield Hall is my home. But I hate this house. You are very young, Miss Eyre. You

cannot understand me.'

'You are right. I don't understand you, sir,' I said.

I stood up.

'Where are you going?' Mr Rochester asked.

'It is late. Adèle must go to bed,' I said.

'Are you frightened of me, Miss Eyre?' Mr Rochester asked.

'No, sir,' I replied. 'But you say strange things, sir.'

Mr Rochester smiled.

'Take Adèle to her bedroom now, Miss Eyre,' he said. 'We will talk again tomorrow.'

––––

After that night, we talked together many times. Mr Rochester was an interesting man. But he was a strange man too. I often thought about him.

'Why does Mr Rochester hate Thornfield?' I asked myself. 'Thornfield Hall is a beautiful place. But Mr Rochester is not happy.'

5
Fire!

It was March. One night, I was in bed. But I was not asleep. The house was quiet. Suddenly, I heard a sound in the corridor outside my room.

'Who's there?' I said. Nobody answered. Then I heard a strange laugh.

I got out of my bed and I went quietly to the door. I listened. I heard another sound. Somebody was walking up the stairs to the top corridor. Then I heard somebody close a door.

'Was that Grace Poole?' I said to myself. 'Yes, it was Grace. Why was she laughing? And why is she walking in the house at night? Is she mad? I must tell Mrs Fairfax about this. I will speak to her now.'

I put on some clothes and I opened the door. There was a candle on the floor outside my room. The candle was burning.

There was thick smoke in the corridor. I went into the corridor. I looked around me. The door of Mr Rochester's bedroom was open. And the smoke was coming from Mr Rochester's room!

I ran into the room.

Stay here, Jane. Open the window. I'll go upstairs.

I sat in a chair by the window. Time passed. At last, Mr Rochester returned.

'Please don't worry, Jane,' he said. 'Grace Poole is a strange woman. But she won't hurt anybody tonight.'

I stood up. 'Goodnight, sir,' I said.

Mr Rochester held my hand. He looked at me and he smiled.

'Thank you, my dear friend,' he said. 'You saved my life tonight, Jane.'

'Goodnight, sir,' I said again.

I went back to my bed. I was very tired. But at first, I could not sleep. Suddenly, I understood something. I loved Mr Rochester! He had smiled at me. He had held my hand. Did he love me? I did not know. But I thought about Mr Rochester for a long time.

———

I did not see Mr Rochester the next day. He did not send for me.

In the evening, I went down to Mrs Fairfax's sitting-room. The housekeeper was looking out of the window.

'The weather has been good today,' Mrs Fairfax said. 'Mr Rochester had a good day for his journey.'

'His journey? Where has he gone?' I asked. I was surprised.

'He has gone to Ingram Park,' Mrs Fairfax replied. 'Mr Rochester will stay there for a week or more. He has many friends. All his friends will be at Ingram Park this week.'

'Will there be any ladies at Ingram Park?' I asked.

'Yes,' Mrs Fairfax said. 'There will be many ladies there. Miss Blanche Ingram will be there. Mr Rochester has known her for many years.'

'Is Miss Ingram beautiful?' I asked.

'She is very beautiful,' Mrs Fairfax said.

'Will Mr Rochester marry her?' I asked.

Mrs Fairfax smiled. 'I don't know, Miss Eyre,' she replied. 'I don't know.'

I was very unhappy. I went up to my bedroom. I looked in my mirror.

'Jane Eyre,' I said to myself. 'You are not pretty. And you are poor. Mr Rochester will never marry you. He will marry Miss Blanche Ingram. She is a rich lady. You are a poor governess. Forget Mr Rochester, Jane Eyre! Forget him!'

6

Guests at Thornfield Hall

Two weeks later, a letter arrived for Mrs Fairfax.

'Mr Rochester will return on Thursday,' Mrs Fairfax said. 'Some of his friends will come here with him. There will be many guests at Thornfield Hall.'

On Thursday evening, Mrs Fairfax, Adèle and I were in Adèle's bedroom. Mrs Fairfax was looking out of the window.

'The guests are arriving now!' Mrs Fairfax said.

I went to the window and I looked out. There were three carriages. Two people were riding horses. Mr Rochester was riding his big black horse. A beautiful young woman was riding a white horse.

Mrs Fairfax pointed to the young woman.

'That is Miss Ingram,' the housekeeper said. Then she went downstairs.

Adèle wanted to go downstairs too.

'No, Adèle,' I said. 'We cannot go downstairs tonight. Mr Rochester is talking to his guests.'

The next day, Mrs Fairfax came into the school-room.

'Mr Rochester wants you to meet his guests tonight, Miss Eyre,' she said. 'Adèle must meet them too.'

Later, Adèle and I went quietly into the sitting-room. And soon, eight ladies came into the room. One of them was tall, dark and very beautiful. She was Blanche Ingram. Adèle ran towards her.

'Good evening, beautiful lady,' she said in French.

'What a pretty little girl!' Blanche Ingram said. Miss Ingram spoke to the other ladies. And she spoke to Adèle. But she did not speak to me.

Half an hour later, the gentlemen came into the room. I looked at Mr Rochester. He saw me, but he did not speak to me.

Miss Ingram pointed at Adèle. 'Why doesn't this little girl live at a school, Mr Rochester?' she asked.

'Adèle learns her lessons at home,' Mr Rochester replied. 'She has a governess.'

'Oh, yes. That small woman by the window,' Miss Ingram said. 'I had many governesses. I hated all of them. They were all ugly and stupid!'

Later, Miss Ingram and Mr Rochester sang some

songs together. Mr Rochester had a fine voice. I listened to the songs, then I left the room. Mr Rochester
followed me.

'What is wrong, Jane?' he asked.

'Nothing is wrong, sir,' I said. 'But I am tired. I am
going to my room. Goodnight, sir.'

'You are tired. And you are unhappy too,' Mr
Rochester replied. 'There are tears in your eyes. Rest
now, Jane. But please come and meet my guests tomorrow evening. Don't forget, my —, don't forget, Jane.'

The guests stayed at Thornfield Hall for two weeks. Every evening, I went to the sitting-room with Adèle. Nobody spoke to me. Mr Rochester and Miss Ingram were always together.

One afternoon, Mr Rochester went to Millcote. He returned late in the evening. I met him at the front door.

'Another guest has arrived, sir,' I told him. 'His name is Mr Mason. He has come from the West Indies.'

Suddenly, Mr Rochester's face was pale. He held my hand tightly.

'Mason. The West Indies. Mason —' he said.

'Are you ill, sir?' I asked.

'Jane, my little friend, I've had a shock,' he said. 'Bring me a glass of wine, please.'

I went quickly to the dining-room. I returned with a glass of wine and I gave it to Mr Rochester.

'What are my guests doing?' he asked.

'They are eating and laughing, sir,' I replied. 'Mr Mason is talking to the other guests.'

'One day, they will all hate me,' Mr Rochester said. 'Now go into the dining-room again. Tell Mason to meet me in the library.'

I gave Mr Mason the message. Then I went to my bedroom. I got into my bed.

Later, I heard Mr Rochester coming up the stairs with Mr Mason. They were laughing and talking. Soon, I was asleep.

7

A Terrible Night

Some hours later, I woke up. A terrible cry had woken me. The moon was bright. Its light was shining through my window. I listened. Then I heard somebody shouting.

'Help! Help! Rochester, help me!'

The voice came from the top corridor.

'Help! Help!'

I got out of bed and I put on a dress and some shoes. I opened my door. All the guests were in the corridor outside the bedrooms. They were all asking questions.

'What happened?' they asked. 'Is there a fire? Who is hurt? Where is Mr Rochester?'

'I am here!' Mr Rochester said. He was walking down the stairs from the top corridor.

'What is wrong, Mr Rochester?' Miss Ingram asked. 'What has happened?'

'Nothing is wrong,' Mr Rochester replied. 'One of the servants has had a bad dream. Go back to bed!'

I went back to my room. But something was wrong. I did not get into my bed. I waited. Soon, somebody knocked on my door. I opened the door. Mr Rochester was standing in the corridor.

'Jane, follow me. Do not make a sound,' Mr Rochester said.

We went up to the top corridor. Mr Rochester

unlocked a door and we went inside a room.

Mr Mason was sitting on a chair in the room. His face was pale. And his shirt was covered with blood! Then I heard a terrible laugh. The sound came from the next room.

'Grace Poole is a madwoman,' I thought. 'Why does Mr Rochester have a mad servant?'

Mr Rochester spoke quietly to Mr Mason.

'I am going to bring a doctor, Richard,' he said.

Then he spoke to me. 'Stay here, Jane. Wash Mr Mason's arm. But do not speak to him.'

Mr Rochester left the room. I washed Mr Mason's arm. We waited for Mr Rochester and the doctor. Mr Mason did not speak to me and I did not speak to him.

After two hours, Mr Rochester returned. The doctor was with him. The doctor looked at Mr Mason's arm.

'She bit me,' Mr Mason said. 'I came up here. I wanted to see her. I wanted to help her. But she bit me!'

'Be quiet now, Richard,' Mr Rochester said quickly.

The doctor put a bandage on Mr Mason's arm. Mr Rochester put Mr Mason's coat round the injured man's shoulders. Then he spoke to me again.

'Run downstairs, Jane. Unlock the small door at the side of the house,' he said. 'We will follow you.'

I went quickly downstairs and I opened the door. Outside the door, a servant was waiting with a carriage. Mr Mason and the doctor came out of the house. They got into the carriage. Then Mr Rochester came out of the house too. Mr Mason spoke to him through the window of the carriage.

'Help her. Be kind to her, Rochester,' he said.

'Yes, I will, Mason,' Mr Rochester said.

The servant drove the carriage away.

'Will you walk in the garden with me, Jane?' Mr Rochester asked. 'I do not want to sleep now.'

'Yes, I will, sir,' I said.

Soon, it was morning. The birds were beginning to sing. The flowers had a sweet smell.

'It has been a strange night, Jane,' Mr Rochester said. 'Were you frightened?'

'I am frightened of Grace Poole,' I said. 'She will hurt you, one day.'

'I am stronger than she is. She will not hurt me,' Mr Rochester said. He looked at me for a few moments. 'Are you my friend, Jane?' he asked me.

'Yes, sir. I will be your friend forever!' I replied.

'Thank you, my dear,' Mr Rochester said. 'I have made mistakes. Now, I want to be happy. That is not wrong, is it, Jane?'

He stopped speaking for a minute. Then he said, 'Go into the house. I'll talk to you tomorrow.'

But the next day, I had a letter from Gateshead Hall, my Aunt Reed's house. The letter was from my Cousin Eliza.

Gateshead Hall

Dear Jane Eyre,
My brother, John, is dead. My mother is very ill. She wants to speak to you. Please come quickly, Jane.
Your cousin,
Eliza Reed

I started the journey to my Aunt Reed's house immediately. I arrived there the next day. My Aunt Reed was very, very ill. She could not move. And she did not speak to me. I wanted to return to Thornfield Hall. I wanted to see Mr Rochester. But Eliza wanted me to stay at Gateshead Hall.

———

After three weeks, my aunt spoke to me at last. She spoke very slowly.

'Are you Jane Eyre?' she asked.

'Yes, Aunt Reed. I am Jane Eyre,' I replied.

'There is a letter for you,' Aunt Reed said. 'It is in my desk. Call Eliza, please. She will get the letter.'

Eliza came into the room. She opened the desk and she gave me a letter.

'Read the letter, Jane,' my aunt said.

The letter had come from Madeira. But it was three years old.

Madeira   October 1831

Dear Madam
I am Jane Eyre's uncle. I am a very rich man. I have no children. One day, Jane will have all my money. Tell her about me. She must write to me.   John Eyre

'I answered that letter,' Aunt Reed said. 'I hated you, Jane. I did not want you to have your uncle's money. I wrote to John Eyre. I wrote, "Jane Eyre is dead. She died at Lowood School." I am sorry, Jane. I was wrong.'

Mrs Reed died that night. I left Gateshead Hall a few days later. I took my uncle's letter with me.

Mr Rochester met me at Thornfield Hall.

'Welcome back to my house,' he said. 'This is your home, Jane.'

'Thank you, sir,' I said. 'I am very happy here.'

Mr Rochester's guests had left. No other visitors came to Thornfield Hall. Every day, Mr Rochester and I talked together. And every day, I loved him more.

8

In the Garden

In June, the weather was hot. One evening, I walked into the garden. Mr Rochester was there too.

'Do you like this house, Jane?' he asked.

'Yes, sir,' I replied.

'Soon, Adèle will go to live at a school, Jane,' he said. 'Then, I will not want a governess here. Will you be sad then, Jane? Will you leave Thornfield Hall?'

'Leave?' I said quickly. 'Must I leave Thornfield?'

'My dear —' Mr Rochester stopped. He was silent for a moment. Then he said, 'I am going to be married soon.'

'Oh, sir,' I said. 'Then I must go far away. Far away from Thornfield. Far away from you, sir.' I started to cry.

'I will always remember you, Jane,' Mr Rochester said. 'Will you forget me?'

'No, sir,' I replied. 'I will never forget you. I don't want to leave Thornfield, sir. I don't want to leave you.'

'Don't leave, Jane,' Mr Rochester said. 'Stay here.' He smiled at me.

'I must not stay here, sir,' I said. 'You are going to marry Miss Ingram. I am poor. I do not have a pretty face. But I have a heart. It is a loving heart, sir!'

'Jane – I am not going to marry Miss Ingram,' Mr

Rochester said. 'She is rich. She is beautiful. You are poor. You are not beautiful. But I want to marry you! Will you marry me, Jane?'

For a moment, I could not speak.

At last, I asked, 'Do you love me, sir?'

'I do,' he replied.

'Then, sir, I will marry you,' I said.

And Mr Rochester kissed me.

'My dearest Jane,' he said. 'Nothing can stop our marriage now. We will be married in a month, Jane!'

We kissed again. Then I said goodnight and I went into the house. I went upstairs to my room.

Later, I remembered my Uncle John Eyre's letter.

'I will write to him in Madeira,' I said to myself. 'I will tell him about my marriage to Mr Rochester. I am very happy. My uncle will be happy too.'

Four weeks passed. Mr Rochester was going to buy me many beautiful things. He was going to give me many presents. But I did not want these things.

'No, Edward,' I said. 'I am not beautiful. I don't want beautiful things. I want you, Edward.'

———

It was the month of July. Two days before our wedding-day, Mr Rochester went away.

'I will return tomorrow,' he said. 'I love you, Jane.'

That night, I went to my bedroom early. My wedding dress and my wedding veil were in my room. I looked at them.

'In two days, I will be Jane Rochester,' I said to myself. Then I went to bed. But I did not sleep well.

The next day, Mr Rochester returned. He looked at me carefully.

'What is wrong, Jane?' he asked. 'Your face is pale. Are you frightened?'

'I had a very strange dream last night,' I said. 'It was a dream about this house. But in my dream, Thornfield Hall had no roof. The walls were burnt. They were black. In my dream, I tried to find you. But you were not in the house.'

'Are you afraid of a dream, Jane?' Mr Rochester asked.

'No, Edward,' I replied. 'But I woke up from my dream. There was a woman in my room. She was tall and heavy. She had long, black hair.'

'The woman was holding a candle,' I said. 'She put

44

the candle by my mirror. She put my wedding veil over her head and she looked in the mirror. Then I saw her face!'

'It was a strange, terrible face, Edward,' I said. 'Suddenly, the woman tore my veil into two pieces. She threw the pieces on the floor!'

'What happened next?' Mr Rochester asked.

'The woman held her candle near my face,' I replied. 'She looked at me and she laughed. Then she went away.'

'This happened in your dream, Jane,' Mr Rochester said.

'It did not happen in my dream, Edward,' I said. 'This morning, my wedding veil was on the floor of my room. It was torn. It was in two pieces!'

'But the woman did not hurt you, Jane,' Mr Rochester said. 'Sleep in Adèle's room tonight, my dear. You will have no more bad dreams.'

9

Mr Rochester's Wife

It was our wedding day. We were going to be married in a church near Thornfield Hall. After the marriage, we were going to travel to London.

I got up early. I put on my wedding dress and I went downstairs. Mr Rochester was waiting for me. At eight o'clock, we walked together to the church. The clergyman was standing by the door of the church.

There were two other people inside the church – two men. They were sitting in a dark corner. I could not see them very well.

The clergyman started to speak. At every marriage, the clergyman asks an important question. He asks the people in the church, 'Is there a problem about this marriage?'

The clergyman spoke loudly. He asked this question and he waited. There was silence for a moment. And then one of the men in the dark corner stood up. He spoke loudly.

'There is a problem. These two people must not be married!' he said.

'There is not a problem!' Mr Rochester said to the clergyman. 'Please go on with the marriage.'

'No, I cannot go on with the marriage,' the clergyman replied. He spoke to the man in the corner.

'What is the problem, sir?' he asked.

Mr Rochester turned and looked at the man.

'Who are you? What do you know about me?' he asked angrily.

'My name is Briggs, sir. I am a lawyer,' the man replied. 'I know many things about you. Fifteen years ago, you were married in the West Indies. Your wife's name is Bertha Mason. She is alive. She lives at Thornfield Hall.'

'How do you know that?' Mr Rochester shouted.

The other man in the dark corner stood up. He walked towards us. It was Richard Mason.

'Bertha Mason is my sister,' he said. 'I saw her at Thornfield Hall in April.'

Mr Rochester's face was pale. For a minute he was silent. Then he spoke quietly.

'It is true,' he said. 'My wife is living at Thornfield Hall. She is mad. Come to the house – all of you! Come and see Mrs Rochester! Come and see the madwoman!'

We all left the church. Nobody spoke.

At Thornfield, Mrs Fairfax and Adèle were waiting for us. They were smiling happily.

'Nobody will be happy today!' Mr Rochester said. 'We are not married!'

Briggs, Mr Mason, the clergyman and I followed Mr Rochester. We followed him up the stairs. He took us to the top corridor. He unlocked a door and we went into a small room. I had seen this room before!

We walked through the room to another door. Mr Rochester unlocked this door and we saw a larger room.

Grace Poole was sitting in the room. But another

woman was there too. She was tall and heavy. Her dark hair was in front of her face. The woman turned and looked at us. I knew that terrible, mad face. I had seen it in my bedroom, two nights before.

The madwoman saw Mr Rochester. She screamed and she ran towards him.

'Be careful, sir!' Grace Poole said.

The madwoman was very strong. She screamed and she hit Mr Rochester. But Mr Rochester held her arms.

'This woman is my wife!' Mr Rochester said angrily.
'I wanted to forget about her. I wanted to marry this
young girl, Jane Eyre. Was I wrong?'

He was silent for a few moments. Then he spoke
quietly.

'Yes. I was wrong,' he said. 'I love Jane Eyre. But I
was wrong. Now, go, all of you. I must take care of my
mad wife!'

———

I went slowly downstairs. Mr Briggs, the lawyer, spoke
to me.

'I am sorry for you, Miss Eyre,' he said. 'You did
nothing wrong. Your uncle, John Eyre, is sorry for you
too. He read your letter. And then he met Richard
Mason in Madeira. Your uncle is dying, Miss Eyre. He
could not come to England. He sent me here. He
wanted me to stop this marriage.'

I did not answer. I went to my room and I locked the door. I took off my wedding dress. I put on a plain black dress. I lay down on my bed.

'I am Jane Eyre today,' I thought. 'I will be Jane Eyre tomorrow. I will never be Jane Rochester. I must leave Thornfield Hall. I must never see Mr Rochester again. My life here is finished.'

Many hours later, I got off the bed. I unlocked my door. Mr Rochester was waiting outside my room.

'You are unhappy, Jane,' he said. 'I am very, very sorry. Jane, we will leave Thornfield. We will go to another country. We will be happy again.'

'I cannot be your wife. I cannot live with you,' I said. 'I must leave you, Edward.'

'Listen, Jane,' Mr Rochester said. 'My father wanted me to marry Bertha Mason. Her family was very rich. I married her. My father was happy. But I was not happy. Bertha was mad, and she was a bad woman. Nobody told me about her. She was married to me, but she met other men. She was drunk every day. She tried to kill me many times.'

'After four years, I brought Bertha here to Thornfield Hall,' Mr Rochester said. 'Then I went away. Grace Poole took care of Bertha. I met other women. One of them was a French singer. She was Adèle's mother. Adèle is my daughter, Jane. But I did not love the French singer. I did not love anybody. I came home to Thornfield Hall. Then you came here and I loved you. I will always love you. Please stay with me, Jane.'

'No, Edward,' I said. 'I am going away. We will be unhappy. But we must not be together. Goodbye, Edward.'

'Oh, Jane! Jane, my love!' Mr Rochester said. 'Don't leave me!'

I kissed Mr Rochester. 'God will help you, Edward,' I said.

Quickly, I went into my room. I put some clothes into a bag. Later, I heard Mr Rochester go into his room. Very quietly, I went downstairs. I opened the small door at the side of the house. I left Thornfield Hall and I walked to the road. It was dark.

Soon, a coach came along the road. I gave all my

money to the driver of the coach. I got into the coach.

———

Many hours later, the coach stopped. It was ten o'clock in the morning.

'You must give me more money now,' the driver said.

'I have no more money,' I said.

'You have no more money? Then you must get out of the coach,' the driver said.

I got down onto the road. The coach moved away quickly. But I had left my bag in the coach.

I looked around me. I was on a cold, empty moor. I was tired and hungry. I walked and walked. I had no money. I had no food. I walked until the evening came. At last, I lay down on the ground. I fell asleep immediately.

10

Moor House

The next morning, I woke late. I walked along the road for many miles. It started to rain. Soon my clothes were wet. I saw no one. I walked on the moor all day. In the evening, I was very tired again.

'I must sleep soon,' I thought. 'Where shall I sleep?'

Then I saw a light. I walked slowly towards it. The rain was falling heavily. But I saw a house near the road. I walked up to the house. I knocked on the door. I waited, but nobody opened the door. I stood outside the house. I was very cold and very tired. I could not move.

'I am going to die here,' I said.

Then I heard a young man's voice. The man was standing behind me.

'No, you will not die at Moor House,' the man said. Then he unlocked the door of the house.

He took me into the house. He took me into a warm sitting-room.

'Please sit down,' he said.

Two pretty young women came into the room.

'Give this poor woman some food, Diana,' the young man said. 'Give her some dry clothes, Mary.'

Then he spoke to me again.

'My name is St John Rivers,' he said. 'These are my sisters, Diana and Mary. What is your name, young woman?'

'My name is Jane — Elliot,' I said. I closed my eyes.

'Jane is very tired,' Diana said. 'She must go to bed now.'

I stayed in bed at Moor House for three days.

———

Diana and Mary Rivers were governesses. They were staying at Moor House for a few days. St John, their brother, was a clergyman. They were very kind to me. Soon, we were good friends.

One day, St John asked me about my life.

'I was a governess too,' I told him. And I told him about Lowood School. But I did not tell him about Thornfield Hall. I did not tell him about Mr Rochester.

'I want to work, St John,' I said. 'Will you help me?'

'I have a plan,' St John said. 'A few miles from here, there is a village. Many of the girls in the village cannot read or write. I am going to pay for a girls' school in the village. But I must find a teacher for these girls.'

'I will teach them, St John,' I said.

'Good!' he said. 'There will be a small house next to the school. You will live there.'

Three days later, a letter arrived for St John.

'Diana, Mary – our Uncle John is dead,' he told his sisters. 'But we will not have any of his money.'

He gave the letter to his sisters. They read it.

'Uncle John was our mother's brother,' Diana told me. 'He was very rich. But he has given all his money to another niece. We do not know her.'

———

Soon, I went to live in the village. I lived in the house next to the school. Every day, I taught the girls. My pupils worked hard. But I was not happy. Every day, I thought about Edward Rochester.

'Does he think about me?' I asked myself.

Four months passed.

One day, St John Rivers came to my house. He was holding a letter. He was worried.

'What is wrong?' I asked.

'I want to ask you three questions, Jane,' he replied. 'Is your name Jane Elliot? Do you have another name? Do you know Jane Eyre?'

I looked at him for a moment. I did not speak.

'I have some news for Jane Eyre,' St John said. 'Jane Eyre was a pupil at Lowood School. And she was a teacher there. Then she was a governess at Thornfield Hall – the home of Mr Edward Rochester.'

'How do you know this?' I asked. 'What do you know about Mr Rochester? How is he?'

'I don't know,' St John said. 'This letter is from a lawyer. The lawyer tells a story about Mr Rochester. Mr Rochester had a mad wife. But he tried to marry Jane Eyre. She left Thornfield. Now this lawyer, Mr Briggs, is trying to find her.'

'I will tell you the truth, St John,' I said. 'My name is not Jane Elliot. My name is Jane Eyre. And I was a governess at Thornfield Hall. I know Mr Rochester. Did Mr Briggs write anything about Mr Rochester?'

'No. The letter is about you, Jane,' St John said. 'Your uncle, John Eyre is dead. John Eyre has given you twenty thousand pounds. You are rich, Jane.'

'But why did Mr Briggs write to you?' I asked.

'My mother's name was Eyre,' St John said. 'She was your father's sister, Jane.'

'Then you, Diana and Mary are my cousins!' I said.

I thought carefully for a moment.

'Write to Diana and Mary,' I said. 'They must come

home. I will give all of you some of Uncle John's money.'

The next day, I wrote to Mr Briggs. I gave St John, Diana and Mary five thousand pounds each. I wrote to Mrs Fairfax too, but she did not reply.

———

Six months passed. I heard nothing from Thornfield Hall. I heard nothing about Mr Rochester.

Then, one day, I was walking on the moor. Suddenly, I heard a voice. There was nobody on the moor. But the voice was calling my name – 'Jane! Jane! Jane!'

'That is Mr Rochester's voice,' I said to myself. Then I shouted, 'I am coming, Edward. I am coming!'

I ran to Moor House. I spoke to my cousins.

'I am going to Thornfield Hall tomorrow,' I told them. I began my journey the next day.

11

My Story Ends

Two days later, I got out of a coach. I was standing on the road near Thornfield Hall. I ran across the fields. Was Mr Rochester at Thornfield? Was he ill?

And then I saw the house. The house had no roof. Its walls were burnt and black. Nobody was living there.

I looked at the burnt, black house. I had seen this before. I had seen it in a dream! I was frightened. Where was Edward Rochester?

I went to the village of Hay. I asked about Thornfield Hall. I asked about Mr Rochester.

'Three months ago, there was a fire at Thornfield Hall,' a man told me. 'The madwoman burnt the house. She was Mr Rochester's wife.'

'Was Mr Rochester in the house?' I asked.

'Yes, he was there,' the man replied. 'He tried to save his wife's life. He went into the burning house. But the madwoman jumped from the roof. She died.'

'Was Mr Rochester hurt?' I asked quickly.

'Yes, he was badly hurt,' the man said. 'He is blind – he can't see. And he has only one hand.'

'Where is he?' I asked. 'Where is he?'

'He is living at Ferndean. It is an old house, about thirty miles away,' the man said.

'Do you have a carriage?' I asked. 'I must go to Ferndean immediately.'

———

I got out of the carriage near Ferndean. I walked to the house. I knocked on the door. A servant opened it. I knew her.

'Oh, Miss Eyre! You have come,' she said. 'Mr Rochester has been calling your name.'

A bell rang in another room.

'That is Mr Rochester's bell,' the woman said. 'He wants some candles.'

There were two candles on a table near the door. The woman lit them and she picked them up.

'Mr Rochester is blind, but he always burns candles in his room in the evenings,' she said.

'Give the candles to me.' I said. 'I'll take them to him.'

I opened the door of Mr Rochester's room. His black-and-white dog was sitting by the fire. The dog jumped up and ran towards me.

'Who is there?' Mr Rochester said.

'Don't you know me, Edward?' I asked. 'Your dog knows me.'

I put the candles on a table. I held Mr Rochester's hand.

'I know that voice. And I know this little hand,' Mr Rochester said. 'Is that you, Jane?'

'Yes, sir, I have found you at last,' I said. 'I will never leave you again.' Then I told Mr Rochester my story.

'Why did you leave your cousins, Jane?' Mr Rochester asked. 'Why did you come back to me? I am blind. I have only one hand.'

'I will take care of you, Edward,' I said.

'But I don't want a servant,' Mr Rochester replied. 'I want a wife.'

'You will have a wife, Edward,' I said. 'I will be your wife. I will marry you. I loved you very much at Thornfield Hall. Now I love you more.'

Mr Rochester and I got married. After a time, his eyes were better. He could see a little. He saw the face of our first child! My dear Edward and I are very happy.

Exercises

Making Sentences

Write questions for the answers.

1 *Where did Jane Eyre grow up?*
   ....
   Jane Eyre grew up at Gateshead Hall.

2 *Why*
   ....
   She lived with her aunt and uncle because her parents were dead.

3 *How*
   ....
   Jane was ten years old in 1825.

4 *What*
   ....
   Her cousins were called John and Eliza Reed.

5 *Did*
   ....
   No, Mrs Reed did not like Jane.

6 *Where*
   ....
   Mrs Reed sent Jane to Lowood School.

7 *Who*
   ....
   Mr Brocklehurst was the owner of Lowood School.

8 *Was*
   ....
   No, Lowood School wasn't a healthy place.

9 *How*
   ....
   Jane stayed at the school for eight years.

10 *When*
   ....
   Jane became a governess in 1833.

Jane Eyre

Complete the information about Jane Eyre in
August 1833.

Date:	August 1833
Name:	
Age:	
Job:	
Subjects:	
Address:	

Choose the Verb

Complete the gaps with the correct verb form from the brackets.

I turned and I ¹......*looked*...... (**looked / looks**) up at my new

home. Thornfield Hall ² .... (**were / was**) a

beautiful house with many large windows. The garden was beautiful too.

After a few minutes, Mrs Fairfax ³............................. (**was

coming / came**) into the garden. She spoke to me.

'Good morning, Miss Eyre,' she said. 'You ⁴.............................

(**were waking / have woken**) early. Miss Adèle

⁵............................. (**is / was**) here. After breakfast, you must

take her to the schoolroom. She [6] .... (**had to / must**) begin her lessons.'

A pretty little girl walked towards me. She spoke to me in French and I [7] .... (**replied / have replied**) in French.

After breakfast, I [8] .... (**took / was taking**) Adèle to the schoolroom. We worked all morning. Adèle enjoyed her lessons and I [9] .... (**am / was**) happy.

In the afternoon, Mrs Fairfax [10] .... (**took / takes**) me into all the rooms of Thornfield Hall. We looked at the paintings and at the beautiful furniture. We [11] .... (**have walked / walked**) along the corridors.

'Come up onto the roof, Miss Eyre,' Mrs Fairfax said. 'You [12] .... (**saw / will see**) the beautiful countryside around Thornfield Hall.'

Multiple Choice 1

Tick the best answer.

1 Who wrote to Jane Eyre from Thornfield Hall?
a ☐ Edward Rochester.
b ☑ Mrs Fairfax.
c ☐ Grace Poole.

2 Who was the owner of Thornfield Hall?
a ☐ Edward Rochester.
b ☐ Mrs Fairfax.
c ☐ Mrs Varens.

3 Adèle was Mr Rochester's ward. What is a *ward*?

a ☐ A child under the protection of an adult.

b ☐ An orphan.

c ☐ A child from another marriage.

4 Mrs Fairfax said: 'Mr Rochester is often away from home.' Why?

a ☐ He often sailed to the West Indies.

b ☐ He had business on the island of Madeira.

c ☐ He did not like Thornfield Hall.

5 Jane heard strange laughter at the top of the house. Who was making the noise? Mrs Fairfax said it was:

a ☐ Adèle Varens.

b ☐ Bertha Mason.

c ☐ Grace Poole.

6 Where did Jane meet Mr Rochester for the first time?

a ☐ In the dining room at Thornfield Hall.

b ☐ On the road to the village of Hay.

c ☐ At Ingram Park.

7 What had happened to Mr Rochester?

a ☐ His dog had bitten him.

b ☐ He had fallen off his horse.

c ☐ He had lost his horse.

8 What did Mr Rochester look like?

a ☐ He was tall and handsome with dark brown hair.

b ☐ He was tall and blond with blue eyes.

c ☐ He had a strong face, dark eyes and black hair.

A Fire at Thornfield Hall

Complete the gaps. Use each word or phrase in the box once.

> this   burning   coming   night   asleep   sound   mad
> smoke   laughing   answered   candle   outside
> opened   heard   open   around   myself   room
> got out of   door   heard   up   put on   quiet   top

It was March. One ¹........night.........., I was in bed. But I was not
²............................. . The house was ³............................. . Suddenly, I
heard a ⁴............................. in the corridor ⁵............................. my room.

'Who's there?' I said. Nobody ⁶... . Then I
⁷... a strange laugh.

I ⁸... my bed and I went quietly to the
⁹..................................... . I listened. I ¹⁰..................................... another
sound. Somebody was walking ¹¹........................... the stairs to the
¹²..................................... corridor. Then I heard somebody close a door.

'Was that Grace Poole?' I said to ¹³... . 'Yes, it was
Grace. Why is she ¹⁴...? And why is she walking
in the house at night? Is she ¹⁵...? I must tell Mrs
Fairfax about ¹⁶... . I will speak to her now.'

I ¹⁷........................... some clothes and I ¹⁸........................... the door.
There was a ¹⁹... on the floor outside my
room. The candle was ²⁰..................................... . There was
thick ²¹..................................... in the
corridor. I went into the corridor. I looked
²²..................................... me. The door of
Mr Rochester's bedroom was
²³..................................... . And the
smoke was ²⁴..................................... from
Mr Rochester's ²⁵.....................................!

Writing

There was a fire in Mr Rochester's bedroom at Thornfield Hall. Jane rescued Mr Rochester.

Look at the pictures and the notes. Write Jane's story about the fire.

1 run into Mr R's room

2 curtains on fire

3 Mr R lying on bed

4 Mr R asleep

I ran into Mr Rochester's room.

Wake up, sir!

5 try to wake Mr R

6 shake him, shout

7 does not wake up

8 see jug of water next to bed

9 pick up jug

10 throw water over bed and Mr R

11 put out flames

12 feel shocked

13 Mr R sits up

14 he asks:

15 I answer:

Multiple Choice 2

Tick the best answer.

1 Jane looked at herself in a mirror. What did she think?
a ☐ 'I am not pretty and I am poor.'
b ☐ 'I will make a good wife for Mr Rochester.'
c ☐ 'I am beautiful and I will be rich.'

2 Mr Mason arrived at Thornfield Hall. Was Mr Rochester pleased?
a ☐ Yes, he was very excited.
b ☐ No, he was rather shocked.
c ☐ No, he was very angry.

3 What happened to Mr Mason?
a ☐ Someone bit his arm.
b ☐ Someone stabbed him.
c ☐ Someone shot him.

4 Aunt Reed showed Jane a letter from her uncle. What did it say?
a ☐ Her parents were not dead.
b ☐ He wanted her to live with him.
c ☐ He wanted to give her all his money when he died.

5 Who wanted to stop Jane and Mr Rochester's marriage?
a ☐ John Eyre.
b ☐ Grace Poole.
c ☐ Jane Eyre.

6 Who were Diana, Mary and St John Rivers?
a ☐ Jane's sisters and brother.
b ☐ Jane's aunts and uncle.
c ☐ Jane's cousins.

7 Jane found Mr Rochester at Ferndean. Why didn't he know her at first?
a ☐ Because he was blind.
b ☐ Because he hadn't seen her for a long time.
c ☐ Because she had changed a lot.

Macmillan Education
4 Crinan Street
London N1 9XW
A division of Macmillan Publishers Limited
Companies and representatives throughout the world

ISBN 978–0–230–03038–1
ISBN 978–1–4050–7616–6 (with CD edition)

This retold version by Florence Bell for Macmillan Readers
First published 1998
Text © Florence Bell 1998, 2002, 2005.
Design and illustration © Macmillan Publishers Limited 2002, 2005

This edition first published 2005

Illustrated by Shirley Bellwood. Map on page 3 by John Gilkes.
Original cover template design by Jackie Hill
Cover illustration by Auguste Macke, Bridgeman Art Library/Getty

These materials may contain links for third party websites. We have no
control over, and are not responsible for, the contents of such third party
websites. Please use care when accessing them.

Although we have tried to trace and contact copyright holders before
publication, in some cases this has not been possible. If contacted we will
be pleased to rectify any errors or omissions at the earliest opportunity.

Printed in Thailand

with CD edition
2018 2017 2016
20 19 18 17 16

without CD edition
2017 2016 2015
15 14 13 12 11